Ghost Town at Sundown

by Mary Pope Osborne
illustrated by Sal Murdocca

A STEPPING STONE BOOK

Random House 🏠 New York

*For Nick Plakias—wonderful friend and
singing cowboy poet*

Text copyright © 1997 by Mary Pope Osborne.
Illustrations copyright © 1997 by Sal Murdocca.
All rights reserved under International and Pan-American Copyright
Conventions. Published in the United States by Random House, Inc., New York,
and simultaneously in Canada by Random House of Canada Limited, Toronto.

http://www.randomhouse.com/

Library of Congress Cataloging-in-Publication Data
Osborne, Mary Pope. Ghost town at sundown / by Mary Pope Osborne ;
illustrated by Sal Murdocca.
p. cm. — (The magic tree house series ; #10) Summary: Their magic tree house
takes Jack and Annie back to the Wild West, where they experience excitement
and danger and try to solve a riddle.
ISBN 0-679-88339-8 (pbk.) — ISBN 0-679-98339-2 (lib. bdg.)
[1. Frontier and pioneer life—West (U.S.)—Fiction. 2. West (U.S.)—Fiction.
3. Time travel—Fiction. 4. Magic—Fiction. 5. Tree houses—Fiction.]
I. Murdocca, Sal, ill. II. Title. III. Series: Osborne, Mary Pope.
Magic tree house series ; #10.
PZ7.081167Gh 1997 [Fic]—dc21 97-7298

Printed in the United States of America   39 40 38

Random House, Inc. New York, Toronto, London, Sydney, Auckland

Contents

Ghost Town
at
Sundown

1

How Wild?

Jack and Annie were sitting on the porch of their house. Annie was gazing down the street at the Frog Creek woods. Jack was reading a book.

"I have a feeling we should check the woods again," said Annie.

"Why?" said Jack without looking up.

"A rabbit's hopping by," said Annie.

"So? We've seen rabbits before."

"Not like this one," said Annie.

"What do you mean?" Jack stood up and looked with her.

He saw a rabbit with very long legs hopping down their street. Soon the rabbit left the sidewalk and headed into the woods.

"He's a sign," said Annie.

"A sign of *what?*" said Jack.

"That Morgan's back," said Annie. She jumped off the porch. "Come on!"

"But what about dinner?" Jack said. "Dad said it would be ready soon."

"Don't worry," said Annie. "You know when we leave in the tree house, time stops."

She ran across their yard.

Jack pulled on his backpack. "Back in ten minutes!" he called through the screen door. Then he followed Annie.

They hurried down their street and into

the Frog Creek woods. The sun was setting above the trees.

"There he is!" said Annie.

The rabbit was standing in a ray of sunlight. When he saw them, he took off.

Jack and Annie followed the rabbit until he vanished behind the tallest tree.

"I told you! See?" said Annie, panting. She pointed up at the tree.

Morgan le Fay was waving to them from the magic tree house high in the branches.

Jack and Annie waved back to her. As always, Jack was very happy to see the enchantress librarian again.

"Come on up!" she called.

Annie and Jack started up the rope ladder. They climbed up to the tree house.

"We followed a strange rabbit here," said

Annie. "Is he your friend?"

"Perhaps," said Morgan. She smiled mysteriously. "I have many odd friends."

"Including us," said Annie.

Morgan laughed. "That's right."

"How are you?" said Jack.

"I'm still having problems with Merlin," said the enchantress, "which leaves me little time to do my real work. But soon you both will become Master Librarians, and that will be a big help to me."

Jack smiled. He was going to be a Master Librarian who traveled through time and space. It was almost too good to believe.

"Are you ready to solve another riddle?" asked Morgan.

"Yes!" said Jack and Annie together.

"Good," said Morgan. "First, you'll need

this for research . . ."

She pulled a book from her robe and handed it to Jack. It was the book that would help them on their journey.

The title of the book was *Days of the Wild West*. On the cover was a picture of a western town on a prairie.

"Oh, wow," said Annie. "The Wild West!"

Jack took a deep breath. *Just how wild?* he wondered.

Morgan reached into the folds of her robe again and pulled out a scroll. She handed it to Annie.

"Read this when the tree house lands," she said.

"Is it the riddle?" asked Jack.

"Yes," said Morgan. "Then you'll only have two more to solve. Are you ready to go?"

Jack and Annie nodded. Annie pointed to the picture on the cover of the Wild West book.

"I wish we could go there," she said.

The wind started to blow.

"Good-bye!" said Morgan. "Good luck!"

The tree house started to spin.

Jack squeezed his eyes shut.

The tree house spun faster and faster.

Then everything was still.

Absolutely still.

Jack opened his eyes.

Morgan le Fay was gone.

A fly buzzed around his head.

2

Rattlesnake Flats

The air was hot and dry.

Jack and Annie peeked outside.

The tree house had landed in a lone tree on a prairie. The sun was low in the sky.

Right in front of them was the town from the cover of the book. In real life it looked empty and spooky.

To one side of the town was a patch of ground with several tombstones.

"That's creepy," said Annie.

"Yeah," said Jack. He took a deep breath.
"What's our riddle say?"

Annie held up the ancient scroll. She unrolled it. Then she and Jack read together:

Out of the blue,
my lonely voice
calls out to you.
Who am I? Am I?

Jack pushed his glasses into place and read the riddle again to himself.

"There must be a mistake," he said. "'Am I?' is written twice."

"Well, I don't hear any voices now," Annie said as she looked out the window.

There were no human sounds at all—only the buzzing of flies and the whistling of the dry wind.

"Let's look at the book," Jack said.

He opened the book. The pages were yellow with age. He found a picture of the town and read the words beneath it out loud:

In the 1870s, Rattlesnake Flats was a rest stop for the stagecoach that carried passengers from Santa Fe, New Mexico, to Fort Worth, Texas. When the creek dried up, everyone left. By 1880, it was a "ghost town."

"Wow, a *ghost* town," said Annie, her eyes wide.

"Let's take a quick look around," said Jack. "So we can leave before dark."

"Right," said Annie. "Let's hurry." She started down the rope ladder.

Jack put the old book into his pack. Then he followed Annie down the ladder.

They stood by the tree and looked about. Tumbleweeds blew across the dry ground.

Suddenly something jumped past them.

"Yikes!" they both said.

11

But it was just a rabbit—a lone, long-legged rabbit hopping past them.

"Hey, he's just like that rabbit we saw at home," said Jack.

"Yeah, that rabbit must have been a sign of things to come," said Annie.

The rabbit hopped across the prairie and out of sight.

"I'd better take notes," said Jack.

He reached into his backpack and took out his notebook and pencil.

He wrote:

rabbits with long legs

"What's that sound?" said Annie.

"What sound?" asked Jack.

"That rattling sound!" said Annie.

Jack looked up. *"What?"* he said.

"There!" Annie pointed to a rattlesnake. It

was about a hundred feet away. It was coiled up and rattling.

Jack took one look at the snake and ran. Annie ran, too. They ran past the graveyard and right into the ghost town.

"I guess that's why this town is called Rattlesnake Flats," said Annie when they stopped.

Jack looked around. The town was hardly big enough to call a town. There was one unpaved street and a few old buildings.

It was quiet, too quiet.

"Look, a store," said Annie.

She pointed to a building. The faded sign said GENERAL STORE. "Let's look inside. Maybe the answer to the riddle is in there."

Jack and Annie stepped onto the porch. The wooden boards creaked loudly. The door had fallen off its hinges. They peeked inside.

The air was thick with dust. Spider webs hung from the ceiling.

"Maybe we shouldn't go in," said Jack.

"But what if the answer's here?" said Annie. "Let's just take a quick look."

Jack took a deep breath. "Okay."

He and Annie tiptoed into the store.

"Look," said Annie. She picked up a pair of rusty spurs.

"Careful," said Jack. He poked at other stuff in the store—an old feed sack, a rusted tin cup, a faded calendar dated 1878.

"Oh, wow," said Annie. She held up two cowboy hats. She put one on and handed the other one to Jack. "For you."

"It's too dusty," said Jack.

"Just blow on it," said Annie.

Jack blew on his hat. A cloud of dust rose up. Jack sneezed.

"Just try it on!" said Annie.

Jack put the hat on. It nearly covered his eyes.

"Boots!" said Annie. She pointed to a row of cowboy boots on a shelf. "There are even some small ones, like our sizes. Here's a pair for you." She handed the boots to Jack.

"They're not ours," he said.

"I know, but just try them on," said Annie.

Jack turned his boots upside down and shook them as hard as he could.

"*What* are you doing?" Annie asked, pulling on another pair of boots.

"Checking for scorpions," Jack said.

"Ja-ack." Annie laughed. "Try them on!"

Jack sighed. He pulled off his sneakers. He

pushed his feet into the boots. He pushed and pushed. The boots were really stiff. Finally he got his feet inside. Then he tried to walk.

"Owww!" he said. "Forget it." He started to pull off the boots.

"What's that?" Annie said.

Jack froze.

"Piano music," said Annie. "Maybe it's the voice in the riddle! Come on!"

Jack threw his sneakers into his backpack and hobbled after Annie.

3

Player Piano

Outside, the sad tune played on.

"It's coming from there," said Annie.

She crept toward a building that had a sign with the word HOTEL on it. Jack limped after her.

Annie slowly pushed open a swinging door. They peeked inside.

The fading daylight lit a piano in the corner of the room. The keys were moving up and down. But no one was there!

17

"Yikes," whispered Annie. "A ghost playing the piano!"

Suddenly the keys were still. The air got very cold.

"No. No way," said Jack. "There's no such thing as a ghost."

"We saw one in ancient Egypt," whispered Annie.

"Yeah, but that was ancient Egypt," said Jack. Even so, his heart raced.

"I'll look it up." Jack pulled out the Wild West book. He found a picture of a piano. He read aloud:

Player pianos were popular in the Old West. The piano played automatically when someone pumped its floor pedals. Later, with the help of electricity, the piano played all by itself.

"Whew." Jack closed the book. "I knew there was an answer," he said. "It must be electric, and somehow it came on."

"I didn't know they had electricity in the Wild West," said Annie.

"They didn't," said Jack.

He looked at Annie. "Oh, man, let's get out of here!" he said.

Jack and Annie backed out of the hotel.

When they got outside, they heard another sound: horse hooves thumping against the hard ground.

A cloud of dust seemed to be moving toward the town. As it got closer, Jack saw three riders. They were herding a small band of horses.

"Hide!" Jack said.

"Where?" said Annie.

Jack looked around wildly. He saw two barrels outside the hotel.

"There!" he said.

Jack and Annie hurried to the empty barrels. Jack climbed inside one and tried to scrunch down. His hat wouldn't fit! He jumped out of the barrel and threw his hat into the hotel.

"Mine, too!" said Annie.

Jack grabbed hers and threw it. Then he scrambled back into the barrel. *Just in time.*

Jack heard the horses thunder into town. He peeked through a crack in the barrel and saw a blur of cowboys and horses go by.

"Whoa!" "Whoa!" "Whoa!" men shouted.

Jack heard the horses come to a halt. They stamped and snorted. All he could see were shadows through the crack.

Dust covered Jack. He had to sneeze. He pinched his nose.

"The creek bed must have dried up!" a cowboy yelled. "This town's a ghost!"

"Yup, it gives me the shivers," said another. "Let's camp over the rise."

Jack *really* had to sneeze now. He pinched his nose tighter. But he couldn't stop the sneeze. He let out a choked "*Ah-choo!*"

"What was that?" someone said.

Just then a loud whinny split the air. Jack saw a beautiful horse rear up.

She had no rider or saddle, just a rope around her neck. She was as red as the sunset. She had a wild black mane and a white star above her eyes.

"We can't keep fighting this one, boss!" a cowboy yelled.

"Yup. She wants her colt," another said. "We shouldn't have left him behind."

"He was too slow," a growly voice said. "We'll sell her when we cross the border."

That's terrible! thought Jack. He knew Annie must be upset, too. He just hoped that she wouldn't jump out of her barrel.

But the cowboys pulled the red horse away. The ground rang from the pounding of hooves as they galloped off.

Jack and Annie stood up. They watched the riders disappear into the dust.

The pounding faded away. All was quiet again, except for the lazy buzzing of flies.

"They were mean to that horse," Annie said in a low, angry voice.

"I know. But there was nothing we could do," said Jack. His boots were killing him. He climbed out of his barrel.

"Man, I have to get these off," he said.

Jack sat down on the porch of the hotel. He grabbed the foot of one boot and pulled.

"Jack," said Annie, "I think there *is* something we can do."

"What?" Jack looked up.

A small horse was running down the road. He was as red as the wild mother horse. He had the same black mane and white star above his eyes.

A rope was around his neck. He looked very lost.

4

Hands Up!

"It's the colt!" said Annie. "He's looking for his mother!"

She ran toward the wild-eyed little horse.

"Wait!" called Jack. "Oh, brother." He pulled the book out of his pack.

He found a chapter titled "Horses of the Wild West." He started reading.

> At the end of the 1800s, over a million wild horses, called *mustangs,* wandered the West. These tough, fast horses were

descendants of runaway Spanish horses.
Mustang herders captured them and
sold them to ranchers. Breaking a wild
mustang took great skill.

Jack turned the page. There was a picture of a herd of horses. Two of them even looked like the beautiful mare and her colt.

"Hey, Annie," Jack called. "You should see this picture."

Annie didn't answer.

Jack looked up.

Annie was trying to get close to the young mustang, but he kept darting away.

"Watch it! He's wild!" said Jack.

Annie was speaking softly to the colt.

She slowly reached out and grabbed the end of his rope. Still talking to him, she led him to a broad wooden post.

"Stop! Don't do anything!" said Jack.

He flipped the pages of his book. He found a section called "How to Treat a Horse."

The basic rules on how to treat a horse are simple: a soft hand, a firm voice, a sunny attitude, praise, and reward.

"I've got the rules!" shouted Jack. "Don't do anything before I write them down!"

Jack pulled out his notebook and pencil. He wrote:

Horse Rules
1. soft hand
2. firm voice
3. sunny attitude
4. praise
5. reward

"Okay, listen—" Jack looked up.

But Annie was already sitting on the colt's back!

Jack froze. He held his breath.

The mustang whinnied and pawed the ground. He snorted and tossed his head.

Annie kept patting his neck and talking softly.

Finally the young horse grew still.

Annie smiled at Jack. "I named him Sunset," she said.

Jack let out his breath.

"Let's go," said Annie. "We have to take him to his mom."

"Are you nuts?" said Jack. "We have to solve our riddle. It'll be dark soon. And those guys were real bad guys, I could tell."

"We don't have any choice," said Annie.

"Oh, brother." Jack knew she wouldn't change her mind. "Let's see what the book says." He read more about mustangs:

> **Wild mustangs live together in families. The bond between a mare and her young is very strong. His sounds of distress or hunger will always bring her to him. A mustang cannot bear to wander alone.**

Jack groaned. He looked at Sunset. The young mustang *did* have a sad look in his eyes.

"Okay, we'll make a plan," he said. "But first I have to get out of these boots."

Jack grabbed one of his boots and pulled.

"Hurry!" said Annie.

"I can't even think in these things!" said Jack.

He huffed and puffed and pulled. Then a deep voice stopped him cold: "Hands up—or I'll shoot!"

Jack let go of his boot. He raised his hands in the air. So did Annie.

A cowboy rode out of an alley. His face was bony and tanned. He was riding a gray horse and pointing a six-shooter.

"I reckon you're the smallest horse thieves I've ever come across," he said.

5

Slim

"We're not horse thieves!" said Annie.

"Well then, what are you doing with my horse here?" he said.

"Some bad guys came through town with his mother," said Annie. "They left him behind because he was too slow."

"Yup, must be the rustlers that stole my last five mustangs," the cowboy said.

"Who are you?" said Jack.

"I'm a mustang herder," the cowboy said.

"They rode through town. Then Sunset showed up all alone," said Annie. "We're taking him to his mother."

"Sunset?" the cowboy said.

"Yup," Annie smiled. "I named him."

The cowboy put away his six-shooter. "Well, you're pretty brave to try and rescue him, Smiley," he said.

"Thanks," said Annie.

Jack cleared his throat. "A mustang needs his family," he said. "The bond between a mare and her young is very strong."

The cowboy looked at Jack. "Whoa, you're pretty smart to know that, Shorty."

"Shorty?" said Jack.

"Every cowpoke's got to have a nickname," said the cowboy.

"What's yours?" said Annie.

"Slim," said the cowboy. "My name is Slim Cooley. And this is Dusty." He patted his horse.

"That fits," said Annie.

Jack agreed. Slim was slim. And Dusty was dusty.

"So tell me," Slim said. "How did you two brave, smart young'uns end up in Rattlesnake Flats?"

Jack caught his breath. He didn't know how to explain it.

"Um . . . the stagecoach," said Annie. "We begged the driver to let us off. But I think we made a mistake."

Slim looked around. "I'll say," he said.

"When the next stage comes through, we're leaving," said Annie.

"I see," said Slim. "Well, I'm going to take

my colt now and find those rustlers. You didn't hear where they were headed, did you?"

"They said they were going to camp over the rise," said Jack.

"Hmm, must be over yonder," said Slim. He looked at a low rise in the distance. The sun was a red ball above it.

"Better get going before dark," he said.

"Can we go with you?" said Annie.

"No, we have to stay here," Jack said quickly. Now that Slim could help Sunset, Jack wanted to look for the answer to the riddle. Plus, he still wanted to take off his boots.

"Shorty's right to be scared," Slim said to Annie. "This is no job for young'uns."

"Scared?" said Jack.

"Oh, please! I want to go," said Annie.

Slim looked at Jack. "And what do *you* want, Shorty?"

For starters, he wanted Slim to stop calling him Shorty. And he wanted Slim to think he was brave.

"Sure, I want to go," said Jack.

"What about your stagecoach?" asked Slim.

"It's not coming until tomorrow," Annie said quickly.

"Well . . . " Slim scratched his chin. "I reckon I could use some brave, smart help. But you have to do everything I say."

"We will!" said Annie. "Can I ride Sunset?"

"I wouldn't say 'yes' to many kids, Smiley, but you seem to have a knack with horses," said Slim. "Now, hang on tight to his mane,

I'll just pull him along behind me."

Slim slipped the rope off the post. Then he held his hand out to Jack.

"Put your foot in the stirrup, Shorty. And grab my hand," said Slim.

Jack did as Slim said. Slim pulled him onto the front of his saddle.

Jack held on to the saddle horn.

"Sit tight," said Slim. "It's not far."

Slim snapped his reins. Dusty took off with Sunset right behind him.

Jack bounced up and down. His boots hurt. The sunlight blinded him.

"Giddy-up!" said Slim.

"Giddy-up!" said Annie.

The horses galloped across the prairie, dust flying from their hooves.

"Ah-choo!" Jack sneezed as he bounced along into the setting sun.

6

Split the Wind

The sky was dark by the time they got to the rise. The wind was cool, almost cold.

"Whoa," said Slim.

Dusty slowed to a halt.

"They're camped down there," Slim said in a low voice. "In that patch of trees."

Jack saw a campfire at the bottom of the slope. He saw the horses gathered in a dark clump. One let out a loud whinny.

"Hear that?" said Slim. "The mare. She

senses Sunset is nearby."

The mare whinnied again.

"Sounds like she's tied to a tree," said Slim. "I think the rest of the herd are loose."

"What's our plan?" whispered Jack.

"Smiley, you stay here and guard Sunset," said Slim.

"Right," said Annie.

"Shorty, you and I ride down near their camp," said Slim. "You keep Dusty quiet while I cut the mare loose."

How do you keep a horse quiet? wondered Jack.

"Once the mare's loose, she'll break for Sunset," said Slim. "Then you and Sunset take off, Smiley."

"Got it," said Annie.

"Then we'll split the wind," said Slim.

What's that mean? wondered Jack.

"Till we get to Blue Canyon," said Slim.

Where's that? wondered Jack.

"All set? Any questions?" asked Slim.

"Nope," said Annie cheerfully.

Yup, about a million, thought Jack.

"Okay, pardners," said Slim. "See ya soon, Smiley. Come on, Shorty."

"Have fun," said Annie.

Fun? thought Jack. *Is she nuts? Our lives are at stake.*

Slim snapped his reins. Dusty started down the rise. Their way was lit by a nearly full moon and a million stars.

Maybe now I can ask Slim some questions, thought Jack.

But just then voices came from the rustlers' camp. They were mean voices, followed by mean laughter.

A chill went through Jack.

Dusty halted.

"This is far enough," whispered Slim. He slipped off of Dusty.

"Keep him here," Slim whispered to Jack, "and keep him quiet."

"Wait—" whispered Jack. He needed more information.

But Slim was gone.

Jack gripped the reins and held his breath. He hoped Dusty wouldn't do anything.

For a moment Dusty was still. But then he snorted and began walking.

Oh, no! thought Jack. He tried to think of the rules on how to treat a horse.

He remembered: *a soft hand, a firm voice.*

He patted Dusty softly.

"Whoa!" he said firmly. To his surprise, Dusty froze and was quiet.

Jack remembered another rule: a sunny attitude. He patted Dusty again. "Don't worry," he whispered. "Everything's going to be fine."

Just then a loud whinny came from the herd of mustangs. They began moving up the moonlit slope.

"Hey! The horses!" a rustler shouted.

A gun went off. Jack ducked.

"Come on, Shorty!" came Slim's voice. Jack looked up. Slim was riding the mare!

Jack was shocked. He had thought that Slim was coming back to ride Dusty.

Instead, Slim rode right past him! As he got close to Annie, she took off on Sunset.

The mare galloped after Sunset. And the band of mustangs galloped after the mare.

Bang! Bang!

Jack snapped the reins. "Go, Dusty!" he said.

Dusty leaped after the mustangs. Jack nearly fell off. He clutched the reins in one hand and the saddle horn in the other.

Bang! Bang!

The rustlers were on their horses now. They were getting closer.

"Hurry!" Jack cried.

Dusty cleared the rise in an awkward leap. Jack started to slip out of the saddle. He let go of the reins and tried to hold on to the saddle horn, but his weight pulled him down. He closed his eyes as he fell to the ground.

Bang! Bang!

Oh, man, thought Jack, *this is the end.*

He opened his eyes. Dusty was looking at him. Jack scrambled up and tried to climb back into the saddle. It was hard without Slim's help.

As Jack struggled, he heard shouts from the rustlers. Their horses gave high-pitched neighs.

Jack looked back.

A shimmering white figure was moving across the top of the rise! The rustlers' horses were panicking and backing away.

Jack didn't have time to think about what he was seeing. He knew it might be his only chance to escape. Using all his strength, he pulled himself into the saddle.

"Go, Dusty, go!" he shouted.

Dusty took off at full gallop over the prairie. Jack held on for dear life as they split the wind.

7

Ghost Story

Jack bounced in the saddle. He felt the cool night wind against his face.

He couldn't tell where they were going. But he trusted Dusty to follow the others.

Finally Dusty caught up with the herd as they began to slow down.

Jack snapped his reins. Dusty came up beside Slim and Annie.

"Howdy!" said Slim.

"Howdy!" said Jack.

"Howdy!" said Annie. "Are you okay?"

Jack pushed his glasses into place. "Yup," he said. "You?"

"Yup," she said.

"That was some good riding, Shorty!" said Slim.

"Thanks," said Jack, smiling. He even liked being called "Shorty" now.

"Where we headed, boss?" Jack asked Slim.

"Blue Canyon," said Slim. "Okay with you?"

"Yup," said Jack.

"This way!" said Slim. He slapped his horse and they all speeded up again.

Slim steered the herd to the left. Soon he led them through a deep, narrow pass.

Finally they came to a boxy open space

surrounded by walls of rock and lit by moon-light.

"We'll corral the mustangs here in Blue Canyon," Slim said.

He got off his horse. He helped Jack down. Annie slipped off Sunset.

"Take him to his ma," Slim told Annie.

Annie led Sunset to the mare. In the moonlight, the two mustangs rubbed against one another and neighed.

As Jack patted Dusty's damp neck, he remembered the last two rules: praise and reward.

"Thanks," he whispered to Dusty. "You were great. You were super great."

Slim unsaddled Dusty, then handed Jack his saddle bags.

"Take those over to that grassy spot.

We'll camp there," he said.

As Jack carried the saddlebags, his boots felt stiff and tight. His legs were sore and wobbly. But he didn't mind.

He threw down the saddlebags and his backpack. Then he flopped himself down. He was *very* tired. Annie joined him.

"They seem so happy to be free and together again," she said, gazing at the moon-lit mustangs.

"Yup," said Jack.

He lay back, using his backpack as a pillow. He looked up at the stars.

"If we just had the answer to the riddle, everything would be perfect," he said.

"Yup," said Annie.

"Hey, Slim," he called. "I have a question for you."

"Shoot," said Slim.

"Do you know the answer to this riddle?" Jack asked. "Out of the blue, my lonely voice calls out to you. Who am I? Am I?"

Slim was silent for a moment, then said, "Sorry, Shorty, don't know that one."

Jack's heart sank. "That's okay," he said. "We don't either."

"I have a question, too," said Annie. "Why does the piano in the hotel play by itself?"

"I *do* know the answer to that one," said Slim.

"What is it?" said Annie.

"It's Lonesome Luke," said Slim. "He's a ghost of a cowboy who wanders the prairie."

Jack sat straight up.

"I saw him! I saw him!" he said. "I just remembered! He scared the rustlers! If he hadn't come, I never would have gotten away!"

"Oh, yeah?" Slim chuckled. "Well, lucky for us, Lonesome Luke sometimes likes to help folks out."

Slim threw his saddle down next to Jack and Annie and sat against it.

"Years ago, Lonesome Luke had a gal who he was just crazy about," said Slim. "She couldn't take the Wild West, though. So she went back east."

"What happened then?" asked Jack.

"Luke went loco. Every night he'd show

up at the hotel and play the piano. He played 'Red River Valley' over and over.

"Then one night he just vanished into the prairie and was never seen alive again. His bones were found a year later. But folks say his ghost returns to the hotel piano to play 'Red River Valley.' It goes like this . . ."

Slim took out a harmonica. He began to play a song. It was the same sad song Jack and Annie had heard in the hotel.

Jack lay back down and listened to the lonesome tune. A coyote howled in the distance. The horses stirred in the dark.

I better take some notes, thought Jack.

But he didn't write a word before he fell asleep. He didn't even take off his boots.

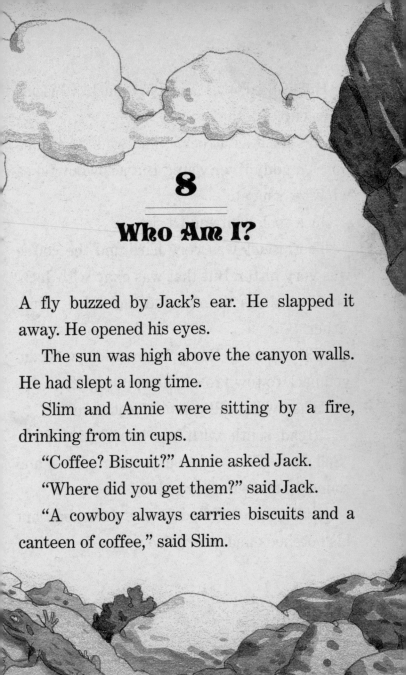

8

Who Am I?

A fly buzzed by Jack's ear. He slapped it away. He opened his eyes.

The sun was high above the canyon walls. He had slept a long time.

Slim and Annie were sitting by a fire, drinking from tin cups.

"Coffee? Biscuit?" Annie asked Jack.

"Where did you get them?" said Jack.

"A cowboy always carries biscuits and a canteen of coffee," said Slim.

He walked over and gave Jack a biscuit and a cup of coffee.

"It's hard as a rock," Slim said. "And bitter as muddy river water. But a cowboy takes what he can get."

Jack took a bite and a sip.

The biscuit was very hard and the coffee was very bitter. But that was okay with Jack. Since cowboys didn't mind, he didn't mind, either.

"I'll saddle up Dusty," Slim said, "and take you back to town to catch your stage."

"Then what will you do?" said Annie.

"Head south with my herd," said Slim. "Sell 'em. Then ride across the plains and round up more mustangs."

While Slim saddled Dusty, Jack took out his notebook and pencil. He wrote:

Cowboy breakfast
bitter coffee
hard biscuits

"Hey, Shorty," called Slim. "What are you doing?"

"Taking notes," said Jack.

"What for?"

"He likes writing things down," said Annie.

"Oh, yeah?" said Slim. "Me too. In fact, I first came out west to write a book. But one thing led to another. The next thing I know, I'm a mustang herder."

"Slim, you *should* write your book," said Annie. "And let the mustangs go free."

"Think so?" said Slim.

They looked at the grazing wild horse.

"I *know* so," said Annie.

"Yup," said Jack. "Your book should be about the Wild West, Slim."

Slim kept staring at his herd. "Maybe you're right," he said. "I could settle in Laramie and write there. Wouldn't have to chase after rustlers anymore."

Slim turned back to Jack and Annie. "Yup, I think I'll be a writer. Let's go. Before I change my mind," he said.

"Yay!" said Annie. "I'll go tell them." She jumped up and ran to the mustangs.

Jack packed his backpack, while Slim packed his saddlebags.

Then Slim and Jack climbed onto Dusty. They rode over to Annie, who was stroking Sunset's neck.

"I told him he's as free as the wind now," said Annie.

"Sounds good," said Slim. "Give me your hand, Smiley."

Slim pulled Annie onto Dusty. She sat in front of Jack.

Slim snapped his reins. Dusty started off.

The sun was hot as Dusty climbed out of the canyon. When they reached the top, they peered down at the canyon floor.

The mustangs pranced playfully, their coats shining in the hazy light.

"They'll find their way out soon," Slim said. "Then cut across the prairie. Yell good-bye to your pal, Smiley."

"Stay with your mother, Sunset!" shouted Annie. "Good-bye!"

Out of the blue, a voice called, *"Bye!"*

Annie gasped. "Who said that?" she asked. "The ghost?"

"Nope," said Jack. "It's just an echo. It's caused by sound bouncing off the canyon walls."

Slim cupped his hands around his mouth. "Who am I?" he shouted.

"Am I?" came the distant voice.

"Oh, man," Jack said softly. "That's the answer . . ."

"To Morgan's riddle!" said Annie.

"Echo!" she and Jack said together.

Jack looked at Slim. "You knew the answer last night," he said.

Slim just smiled and snapped his reins. "Let's go, pardners," he said.

9

Lonesome Luke

The sun was low in the sky when they reached Rattlesnake Flats.

"Just let us off in front of the hotel," said Annie.

"You sure the stage is coming through here?" said Slim.

"Yup," said Jack and Annie together.

In front of the hotel, Slim got down from Dusty. Then he helped Jack and Annie down.

"I hope you'll come to Laramie and visit

me," said Slim. He winked. "I might be needing some help on my book."

"Sure," said Annie.

Slim climbed back on Dusty. He looked down at Jack.

"You know, Shorty," he said, "you might be short, but you're mighty tall in the brains."

"Thanks," said Jack.

"And, Smiley," Slim said. "Your great courage is nothing to smile about."

"Thanks," said Annie.

"Good luck with your writing, Slim," said Jack.

"I'm grateful to you both for steering me straight," said Slim. "I promise I'll thank you someday."

"Really?" said Annie.

"A cowboy never goes back on his word,"

said Slim. Then he snapped his reins, and Dusty loped down the street.

"Bye, Slim!" yelled Annie.

Slim Cooley turned one last time. He waved his hat. "So long, pardners!" he called.

Then he rode off into the sunset.

Jack let out a deep sigh. "Okay. I'm ready to take my boots off now," he said.

"Me too," said Annie.

They sat down on the porch of the hotel. They started pulling off their boots.

"There!" Jack got them both off.

He wiggled his toes. He took his sneakers out of his pack and put them on. Annie put hers on, too.

"Man, sneakers never felt so good," said Jack.

Suddenly the sound of a piano drifted through the air.

"Lonesome Luke!" said Annie.

Jack grabbed his pack. He and Annie crept across the porch. They pushed open the swinging door.

The piano was playing "Red River Valley." Sitting on the piano stool was the dim but shimmering shape of a cowboy.

Just then the ghost of Lonesome Luke looked at Jack and Annie. He waved a shimmering hand.

Jack and Annie waved back.

Then the ghost of Lonesome Luke faded away. Cold air wafted past Jack and Annie. They both shivered.

"Oh, man, let's go," breathed Jack.

They leaped and dashed up the dusty road. They ran across the cracked ground and past the graveyard. They ran until they reached the tree with the Magic Tree House in it.

Annie grabbed the rope ladder.

She hurried up and Jack followed. They were out of breath when they got inside the tree house.

Annie grabbed the ancient scroll. She unrolled it.

"Yay!" she said.

The scroll had one glowing word on it:

ECHO

"We got it right!" said Annie.

Jack grabbed the Pennsylvania book. He pointed to a picture of the Frog Creek woods.

"I wish we could go there!" he said.

The wind started to blow.

The tree house started to spin.

It spun faster and faster.

Then everything was still.

Absolutely still.

10

Echo from the Past

Jack and Annie looked outside.

The sun had slipped behind the trees of the Frog Creek woods.

Annie still held the ancient scroll. She put it in the corner, next to the scroll from their ocean trip.

"Just two more to go," she whispered.

"Yup," said Jack. He unzipped his pack. He pulled out *Days of the Wild West*. He put it on top of a stack of books.

"Ready?" he said.

Annie was staring at the books. Her mouth dropped open.

"What's wrong?" asked Jack.

Annie just kept staring.

"Have you gone nuts?" said Jack.

Annie pointed at the Wild West book.

"Read the cover," she said.

Jack picked the book up. He read the title aloud: *"Days of the Wild West."* He looked at Annie. "So?"

"Keep reading," said Annie.

The author's name was below the title. It was in smaller letters. Jack read: "Slim Cooley."

Jack gasped. *His* mouth dropped open. He and Annie stared at the words for a long moment.

"Oh, man," whispered Jack. "We were using Slim's book. The book he wrote after he left us!"

Jack and Annie shook their heads with wonder.

Jack opened Slim's book. He looked at the title page. At the bottom of the page, he read: *Texas Press, Dallas, 1895.*

Jack turned the page. He read the dedication:

WITH THANKS TO SMILEY AND SHORTY,
TWO STRANGERS WHO CHANGED MY LIFE

Jack looked at Annie. "Slim dedicated his book to us," he said.

"Yup," said Annie. She smiled.

Jack placed Slim's book back on the stack of books.

Then he and Annie left the tree house and climbed down the ladder.

As they started through the woods, the trees were alive with bird sounds. The air felt soft and moist.

"Frog Creek seems so peaceful," said Jack. "No rattlers, no rustlers, no ghosts."

"Yeah, but no Slim Cooley either," said Annie sadly.

"I know," said Jack. "But when we read his book, it's like he's still talking to us."

"Oh, right," said Annie. "You mean it's like an echo from the past?"

"Yeah," said Jack softly. "Wow."

Just then, out of the blue, a voice called, "Jack! Annie!"

"It's Dad!" said Annie.

"Coming!" she and Jack shouted.

Then they ran all the way home, through the long shadows of the setting sun.

Here are the words to
RED RIVER VALLEY,
the traditional cowboy song that
Lonesome Luke played on the piano.

From this valley they say you are going.
I shall miss your sweet face and bright smile.
For they say you are taking the sunshine
That has brightened my pathway awhile.

Refrain (after each verse):

Come and sit by my side if you love me.
Do not hasten to bid me adieu.
For remember the Red River Valley
And the cowboy who loved you so true.

There never could be such a longing
In the heart of a poor cowboy's breast.
As dwells in this heart you are breaking
While I wait in my home in the West.

Do you think of this valley you're leaving,
Oh, how lonely and dreary it will be?
Do you think of the kind hearts you're grieving,
And the pain you are causing to me?

From this valley they say you are going.
I will miss your bright eyes and sweet smile.
For they say you are weary and tired
And must find a new range for a while.

Where have *you* traveled in the

MAGIC TREE HOUSE

The Mystery of the Tree House
(Books #1-4)

❑ **Magic Tree House #1, Dinosaurs Before Dark**
in which Jack and Annie discover the tree house and
travel back to the time of dinosaurs.

❑ **Magic Tree House #2, The Knight at Dawn**
in which Jack and Annie go to the time of knights
and explore a medieval castle with a hidden passage.

❑ **Magic Tree House #3, Mummies in the Morning**
in which Jack and Annie go to ancient Egypt and get
lost in a pyramid when they help a ghost queen.

❑ **Magic Tree House #4, Pirates Past Noon**
in which Jack and Annie travel back in time and meet
some unfriendly pirates searching for buried treasure

The Mystery of the Magic Spell
(Books #5-8)

Magic Tree House #5, Night of the Ninjas, in which Jack and Annie go to old Japan and learn the secrets of the ninjas.

Magic Tree House #6, Afternoon on the Amazon, in which Jack and Annie explore the rain forest of the Amazon, and find crocodiles, giant ants, and flesh-eating piranhas.

Magic Tree House #7, Sunset of the Saber-tooth, in which Jack and Annie go back to the Ice Age—the world of woolly mammoths, sabertooth tigers, and a mysterious sorcerer.

Magic Tree House #8, Midnight on the Moon, in which Jack and Annie go forward in time and explore the moon in a moonbuggy.

The Mystery of the Ancient Riddles
(Books #9–12)

❏ **Magic Tree House #9, DOLPHINS AT DAYBREAK,** in which Jack and Annie arrive on a coral reef, where they find a mini-submarine that takes them underwater into the world of sharks and dolphins.

❏ **Magic Tree House #10, GHOST TOWN AT SUNDOWN,** in which Jack and Annie travel to the Wild West, where they battle horse thieves, meet a kindly cowboy, and get some help from a mysterious ghost.

❏ **Magic Tree House #11, LIONS AT LUNCHTIME,** in which Jack and Annie go to the plains of Africa, where they help wild animals cross a rushing river and have a picnic with a Masai warrior.

❏ **Magic Tree House #12, POLAR BEARS PAST BEDTIME,** in which Jack and Annie go to the Arctic, where they get help from a seal hunter, play with polar bear cubs, and get trapped on thin ice.

Read all the Magic Tree House books!

Available wherever books are sold...

OR

**You can send in this coupon (with check or money order)
and have the books mailed directly to you!**

❏ Magic Tree House #1, DINOSAURS BEFORE DARK
(0-679-82411-1) $3.99

❏ Magic Tree House #2, THE KNIGHT AT DAWN
(0-679-82412-X) $3.99

❏ Magic Tree House #3, MUMMIES IN THE MORNING
(0-679-82424-3) $3.99

❏ Magic Tree House #4, PIRATES PAST NOON
(0-679-82425-1) $3.99

❏ Magic Tree House #5, NIGHT OF THE NINJAS
(0-679-86371-0) $3.99

❏ Magic Tree House #6, AFTERNOON ON THE AMAZON
(0-679-86372-9) $3.99

❏ Magic Tree House #7, SUNSET OF THE SABERTOOTH
(0-679-86373-7) $3.99

❏ Magic Tree House #8, MIDNIGHT ON THE MOON
(0-679-86374-5) $3.99

❏ Magic Tree House #9, DOLPHINS AT DAYBREAK
(0-679-88338-X) $3.99

Subtotal...$ 4.99

Shipping and handling ....$ 3.00

Sales tax (where applicable) _____

Total amount enclosed ....$ _____

Name _____

Address _____

City _____ State _____ Zip _____

Prices and numbers subject to change without notice. Valid in U.S. only.
All orders subject to availability. Please allow 4 to 6 weeks for delivery.

Make your check or money order (no cash or C.O.D.s)
payable to Random House, Inc., and mail to:
Magic Tree House Mail Sales, 400 Hahn Road, Westminster, MD 21157.

Need your books even faster? Call toll-free 1-800-793-2665
to order by phone and use your major credit card.
Please mention interest code 049-20 to expedite your order.

Look for these other Random House books
by Mary Pope Osborne!

Picture books:

Molly and the Prince
Moonhorse

For middle-grade readers:

American Tall Tales
One World, Many Religions

And available spring 1998,
the Spider Kane mysteries!

*Spider Kane and the Mystery Under
the May-Apple (#1)*
*Spider Kane and the Mystery at
Jumbo Nightcrawler's (#2)*